Back To the Past

Night Time Dialogs That Make You Think

This is a work of fiction. This book's story and characters are fictitious. Certain well-known organizations may be mentioned, but are mentioned solely in a fictitious way for the purpose of this fiction story.

ISBN: 9798598023846

AF580995

Dedication

This book is dedicated to my incredibly delightful granddaughter, Sadie, who, I love dearly, and hope can live in a world even better than the world in which I grew up.

Acknowledgements

I would like to thank friends and family who supported me throughout my endeavor of writing this book. They've provided tremendous support providing encouragement, editing and illustrations. And they've endured more questions than a anyone should ever be subject to.

Preface

While I hope this book will be entertaining, its primary purpose is to be thought-provoking and to be a catalyst for conversations that need to happen. You can obviously read this book alone. But I think it would be much more useful if it is read and discussed in pairs or groups. That's where discovery and enlightenment are most likely to emerge.

Table of Contents

Table of Contents 3

Chapter 1 4

Chapter 2 8

Chapter 3 14

Chapter 5 22

Chapter 6 27

Chapter 7 32

Chapter 8 38

Chapter 9 42

Chapter 10 45

How to sign the Declaration of an American Patriot 54

Rules of Engagement 56

Declaration of an American Patriot 57

My Vision 60

Chapter 1

PaPa: Well, Sam. How's my 10-year-old grand girl? Did you have a Happy Birthday? This is a gift from me and MaMa?

Sam: I'm having a wonderful birthday with y'all. Thanks so much for the shoes. I really needed a new pair. I've been getting sand and pebbles in my old shoes and it's making my feet sore. Where in the world did you find new shoes?

PaPa: On my way to Farmerville, I stopped and helped Jimbo raise his hut so it wouldn't flood again. In return, he gave me a pair of shoes he had bought for his daughter, Liz.

Sam: But PaPa! That's not fair to Liz. Please give the shoes back. I really don't need them. I'm plenty happy spending my birthday with you and MaMa. I don't need anything else.

PaPa: Now, now Sam. I'm sorry to say this, but Liz caught a really bad virus and is no longer with us. So Jimbo doesn't need the shoes anymore. He was very, happy to know you'd be getting some good use out of her shoes. That made his day.

Sam: Ok. Well, the next time you get provisions, can you bring back some extra flour? I think I'll bake Jimbo a loaf of bread. Would you deliver it for me?

PaPa: How 'bout if we deliver it together? He'd like that very much. Anything interesting happen at school today?

Sam: You bet! MaMa told us a story about some impossible land not so far from here. But PaPa. I think MaMa's gone cuckoo. She didn't finish the story. She's gonna make US finish the story at school, tomorrow.

MaMa: I heard that. Your grandmother is not cuckoo. Or at least no more cuckoo than PaPa.

PaPa: Watch out, MaMa. That kinda talk'll get you in trouble.

MaMa: YOU better watch out, PaPa. This is MaMa you're dealing with. And NO, I did not FORGET to finish the story. I just want to see how the students in class will end the story. It's a great way to get to know each other better.

PaPa: Wow! That's a great idea. If I have time tomorrow, I'll sneak in the class and listen to you guys end the story.

Sam: I'm not a GUY PaPa.

PaPa: Of course, you're not a guy. That's just a manner of speaking. You're a beautiful little girl. Oops, a beautiful BIG girl now. MaMa, would you mind telling us your story again, or should I say the beginning of your story. Sam has heard it, but I'm in the dark.

MaMa: I'd be happy to. Y'all get comfortable. Ready?

PaPa: Yup!

Sam: Me too!

MaMa: Here we go! Not so long ago in a land not so far from here, life was very, different than it is today. You could get light in your house by simply flipping a switch. It was like having daylight in your house whenever you wanted. You could get fire on your stove by just turning a knob. There was no need to gather firewood. This made cooking so much easier. You could get clean water by just lifting a lever – even hot water if you wanted!

You could get rid of your poop by pushing down on lever. Whoosh! It was gone. You could talk to almost anyone you wanted anywhere in the world using a device called a phone. You could even SEE them talking. You could travel hundreds of miles in ONE DAY in a comfortable car – even in the rain.

Sam: What's a car?

MaMa: It's like the wagon we take to town to get provisions. But it's got a cover to keep the rain out and doors on the side to keep people in and animals out. And you don't even need a mule to pull it. You just push a pedal and away you go!

Sam: That's too crazy to even imagine.

MaMa: Hey! It could happen.
You could even FLY thousands of miles to places all around the world in a single day.

Sam: C'mon MaMa. People can't fly.

MaMa: But Sam, I'm the teacher and this is MY story. And if I say pigs fly in my story – then pigs will fly in my story. But wait! There's more. There was this thing called the internet. The internet was kind of like a courier in a box – or should I say a whole bunch of couriers. People would put news on the internet, and it was delivered instantly! When I say instantly, I mean less than a second. News from all over the world came to you, sometimes as it was happening, instead of waiting weeks or even months to hear the news from a courier. Sometimes, you could even get the news before it happened.

Sam: How can you get news that hasn't happened yet?

MaMa: EXACTLY! News was getting to everyone so fast that some people made careless mistakes. Others put out fake news just to get attention. Some even put out fake news to hurt others. Soon there was so much news being reported that most people couldn't tell what news was real and what news was fake. And because of all this confusion people stopped trusting each other.

It got so bad that many people started losing confidence in the government and the police.

Sam: You nuts, MaMa. How can you think up such crazy stuff?

MaMa: I guess I'm just overly imaginative.

Sam: So, what happened next?

MaMa: Some people got really, angry because of what they saw on the news, even though lots of times the news was wrong. Some got so mad, they became thugs and started breaking the law. They started robbing and stealing. They tore up homes and businesses and even burned some. They blocked streets and fought the police. They even destroyed historic monuments of some of the most important people in the history of the country. Man, we are talking about a horrible mess.

Sam: That's just not right. It makes me sad just thinking about it.

MaMa: Well, it just gets worse. There were instances where people got shot and died. Sometimes, this was by accident, but whether this was on purpose or by accident people still died needlessly.

Sam: I don't like this story.

MaMa: Then maybe you can come up with a happy ending for the story in class tomorrow. Think about it! But get some sleep now.

PaPa: You stay warm under your blanket and I'll blow the candles out for you.
Goo-oo-oo-oo-ood night, Sam.

Sam: Good night PaPa. Good night MaMa.

MaMa: Good night, Sam.

Chapter 2

Sam: It's getting chilly in here, PaPa.

PaPa: You get ready for bed and I'll throw more wood on the fire.

Sam: Thanks, PaPa!

MaMa: Thanks for stoking the fire, PaPa. I've got some hot cocoa for you and Sam.

PaPa: Yeah! That's great. Oooh! And you brought cookies, too. Five for me and one for Sam? Huuum! You should've brought a cookie for yourself MaMa.

MaMa: That's two cookies a piece. And you'd better not eat anyone else's cookies if you know what's good for you.

PaPa: MaMa, you know Sam wouldn't eat my cookies.

MaMa: Cut it out, PaPa. I know you WOULD eat Sam's cookies and you'd better not if you know what's good for you.

PaPa: Rocka-socka-bocka.

MaMa: Stop grumbling PaPa. Sam, you sure look warm in your jammies.

Sam: I sure am. I'll be even warmer after I drink a cup of your hot cocoa. Thanks, MaMa. I can't wait to tell PaPa about the different endings to your story. But I think we should let PaPa go first.

MaMa: That's a GREAT idea. Well, PaPa? Looks like the spotlight's on you!

Sam: What's a spotlight? I don't see anything on PaPa. Not even any hair.

PaPa: Hey! No picking on my shiny head. In the old days, when someone would sing in front of a crowd, somebody would shut of all the lights in the room except one single light that would shine on the singer. Since the light would shine only on one spot, the light became known as the spotlight.

PaPa winds up an old emergency flashlight and shines it on MaMa.

PaPa: Spotlight's on you, MaMa. Now sing!

MaMa: No way! I don't want to hurt anyone's ears. PaPa, how about if you stop beating around the bush and give us your ending to the story.

PaPa: OK! OK! To begin with, I think it is a crazy story. Only MaMa could think up such nonsense? But, if it ever did happen, I think all hell would break loose. I think the peaceful citizens would start fighting back and it would be difficult for the cops to see who the good guys were and who was bad. I think the bad guys would get bolder to intimidate the police and the police would have no choice but to get stricter in order to protect people and property. Then the mob would accuse police of getting too strict and the mob would retaliate by getting even more aggressive and resistant. And the police would have to get even stricter. **The cycle will have begun!**

Sam: What do you mean "the cycle will have begun"?

PaPa: The cycle of criminals getting worse and cops having to get tougher, making the criminals retaliate harder. Then the cops having to get tougher and the criminals retaliate even harder. Then the cops having to get tougher and the criminals retaliate even harder. Then this cycle goes on and on and on and gets worse and worse and worse until it hits the fan.

MaMa: Very interesting. What do you think Sam?

Sam: I can't stand PaPa's ending. It stinks.

PaPa: Don't blame me! MaMa made up the silly story. Y'all asked me to give an ending, so I just made one up to please y'all.

MaMa: Well, we didn't ask for such a rotten ending. Maybe Sam has a better ending. Sam?

Sam: Can I give Ted's ending first?

PaPa: Sure.

Sam: Ted said he thought it would be too dangerous to be a policeman and most of them would quit. Then, without the policeman to help protect the fireman and ambulances, we'd lose them, too. Then, people would move away from big cities to avoid the burning buildings and being hurt by thugs. Then, everyone would be living in small villages away from the rest of the world and we'd be living like wild animals live.

MaMa: Wow! That's kinda how we live now, huh? Small villages. Away from the big cities as much as possible. Ted really put some thought into that one. I'm impressed.

PaPa: Ditto!

Sam: I thought a lot about it too. I love our nighttime chats. We talk about what's on our minds. Seems like if everyone around the world could do this, we'd have a whole lot less violence. For my ending, everyone realized the world was getting messed up, so they got together and started speaking calmly with each other and understand each other's point of view. Then they were able to resolve their differences and everyone lived happily ever after.

PaPa: That would be the best ending ever, Sam. But if that were the case, why didn't people do this before everything collapsed in the first place?

Sam: Good question. I don't know why people didn't do that in the first place. Maybe it's because they all yelled and fussed at each other instead of talking calmly like we do. They probably didn't even listen to each other. Maybe it could have all been avoided if they had had chats like we have all around the country. They sure could have used that internet thing you were talking about.

PaPa: It seems to me like either of these scenarios could happen.

Sam: I wonder which one these would happen? Or if something else would happen?

MaMa: Maybe it's all up to us. Maybe we have to BE the change. I don't think the land in the story just happened. I think someone, many someones, made it happen. So, if we want to live in a land where people talk and resolve their differences peacefully, maybe WE have to get the ball rolling.

Sam: What do you mean get the ball rolling?

MaMa: That's a figure of speech. You can start with a small snowball. Roll it down the hill and it'll get bigger and bigger. Likewise, we can start with small discussions, like the snowball. We can sit down and see what we agree on and what we disagree on. Then, just like the snowball gets bigger and bigger, we understand each other more and more. Then, if we understand each other, we can begin to resolve more and more problems peacefully.

Sam: Why do you say, "US" and "WE"? You must mean the people in the story!?

PaPa: Should we tell her?

MaMa: Why not? But she'll never believe it.

Sam: Believe what?

MaMa: Sam! Sit down. This is going to be really hard to believe.

Sam: I am sitting down. And it can't be **that** hard to believe if it's true. What is it?

PaPa: About the story MaMa started. Well Sam. As unbelievable as it may sound, it's a true story. That's how the world really was 30 years ago. You really could get light in your house by flipping a switch and fire on your stove by turning a knob. You really could get clean water by lifting a lever and get rid of your poop by pushing a lever. You really could talk to people thousands of miles away and travel hundreds of miles a day with ease. Yes, you could even fly all around the world.

Sam: Cut it out! You're teasing me.

PaPa: No! We're not teasing. That was probably the best time to live that ever was. Life was pretty, easy for most people in America. Surviving was so much easier than it is today. Most people took what they had for granted. They didn't appreciate the good life they had. Some people got greedy. Others were complacent. And some got jealous that their life wasn't as good as they thought it should be. So, now, it's kinda like we've gone back to the past. **W-a-a-a-a-y back!**

Sam: But they had light without candles. They didn't have to gather firewood and water. They could poop without going outside in the cold and freezing their butt off. How could they not be happy?

PaPa: I guess it's all about what you think happiness is. I think happiness is how closely your life mirrors how you think life should be. Take someone who has just about everything you can imagine. If he thinks he should have even more, he'll be unhappy with what he has. But if that same person compares himself to those who don't have it as good as him, he will probably be happy. There's always gonna' be those better off than you and those worse off than you.

Sam: That makes sense.

PaPa: Good. Now let me complicate it just a little. When we see someone, we only perceive how well off they are. We don't know what their life is really like. They may appear to be very, happy. But, in reality, they may not be so happy. So, remember the moral of the story. Don't compare yourself to anyone else. If you compare yourself to someone you think has it better off than you, you gonna be sad girl.

Sam: Wow! That's deep. I'm gonna have to sleep on it. It seems too simple.

PaPa: How about if I complicate it even more. One of the best ways to make yourself happier is to help make someone else happier.

Sam: Good night, PaPa. My head is too full to think.

PaPa: Okay! I'll stop rambling.

MaMa: Bologna, PaPa! You'll stop rambling when dogs stop barking. Good night, Sam.

PaPa: I guess I was just born a rambling man! Good night, Sam. Sweet dreams.

Sam: Good night, MaMa. And PaPa, you can ramble to me whenever you want. I love it. Good night.

Chapter 3

Sam: You know, PaPa, I been thinking. People must'a been real sad about something if they started steeling and burning and killing? What were they so sad about?

PaPa: That's the million-dollar question. I'm no expert. I can only tell you what I saw on the news. But there was a lot of stuff happening that I need to explain.

Sam: I'm all ears. Kinda like you since you don't have any hair.

PaPa: You had to pick on my bald head, huh?

Sam: giggle

PaPa: Getting back to the subject. There was this group call Black Lives Matter.

Sam: But don't ALL lives matter. Why not just call the group ALL Lives Matter?

PaPa: According to sources I've heard, it was called Black Lives Matter because the group insisted that white cops were killing black people with no good reason.

Sam: What's a cop?

PaPa: Cops is a word used for people hired by the government to protect the people. When I say government, it's kind of like what we call elders today. The government was a group of people the tribes chose to make the rules that everyone was supposed to live by. These rules are supposed to be there to make life easier and fair for everybody. The cops were the people the government hires to make sure everyone obeys those rules.

Sam: Why were the white cops killing the black people?

PaPa: I believe in every group of people – elders, cops, hunters, teachers, preachers, doctors, builders – there's gonna be a few bad apples. But, with the news being the way that it was, there was a lot of interest in seeing the bad stuff. Not so much interest in seeing the good stuff. You know – same old, same old. Say you had 1000 cops and 5 of them end up killing black guys, you'd likely only see the 5 bad cops in the news. So, all you ever see about cops is bad stuff. You never see the 995 good cops and all the indispensable work they did. This gave the cops a bad rap in many people's eyes. The situation is even worse. Out of those 5 "bad cops", many of their acts may have been justified. Maybe, the suspect pulled a gun on the cop or was a risk to others. All too often the cop has to make a split-second decision. And his decision may determine whether he will live or die and whether innocent citizens will live or die.

Sam: Why were only the "bad" cops on the news and not the good cops?

PaPa: I guess everybody wanted to know what was going wrong and assumed everything else was just fine. It's kinda like when you check on the chickens for me. You tell me which ones are having problems. But you don't say anything about the healthy ones. Say you saw 2 sick chickens and 200 healthy chickens. How long would it take you to tell me about the healthy ones. I wouldn't have time to listen to them all. Same thing with the cops. If you reported on all the good cops, it would take so long you probably wouldn't even notice the bad cops in the mix.

Sam: Well, I guess you can't blame the news. Hu-u-um? So, what should the news people do?

PaPa: Excellent question. I'll have to think about that one. But the problem spirals out of control like a tornado. Now, you had a bunch of black people, and even some white people, saying that the white cops are bad. So, say you have 1000 of these people in Black Lives Matter protesting and 5 of them start steeling and vandalizing. You see these 5 people in the news, and it gives Black Lives Matter a bad name. Now, white cops and Black Lives Matter protesters are all getting a bad name. So, white folks despise the Black Lives Matter supporters and Black Lives Matter folks loath the White Cop Supporters. And since everybody supports somebody, everybody dislikes somebody, and everybody is disliked by somebody. Trust and cooperation disappear like poop down the toilet. We're talking bad. REEEAAALLY BAD!

Sam: Sounds like they're gonna need a whole lot of talking to clear that mess up.

PaPa: You bet! And a whole lot of listening. But everyone is convinced they are right. Kinda like everybody knows the best way to make scrambled eggs. If this is ever to be resolved, both sides need to understand the other side's point of view. And before this can happen, we gotta talk about slavery.

MaMa: I hate this subject. I'll take this as an opportunity to make us all some hot chocolate.

Sam: YEAH! YEAH! YEAH!

PaPa: I'd love a cup of hot chocolate.

MaMa: I knew you wanted some. You're nothing but a big chocoholic.

PaPa: And proud of it. But back to the slaves. Slavery is when one person owns another person. A slave owner owns a slave. Kinda like you'd own a horse or a dog. Slave owners made their slaves work hard without paying them. Slave owners often treated their slaves poorly. Most slaves probably woke up in the morning and worked all day long until they went to bed. They probably thought all day along about how it must feel to be free like the people who owned them. To come and go as you please. To go to school and learn new stuff. To go on picnics and vacations with their friends and family. That's all stuff slaves couldn't do. Since they were considered property, like a piece of furniture, all they could do was what their owner allowed them to do.

Sam: Why would anyone want to be a slave?

PaPa: No one would ever WANTS to be a slave. These people were caught like wild animals, taken from their home, and forced to be slaves. They had no choice, and if they tried to escape, they were usually beaten really bad or worse. I can't imagine anything worse than being forced into slavery. They had little or no chance to ever escape. It's hard to imagine what it must have been like. I don't think we can. I don't think we want to. But it's as true as it is unthinkable.

Sam: They probably thought all day long about their family knowing they'd never see them again. That makes me want to cry.

MaMa: If you think it makes YOU want to cry; imagine how you would feel if you knew your ancestors were slaves. Actually, if you could go far enough back – there's a good chance you did have some ancestors who were slaves.

Sam: My what?

PaPa: Your ancestors. That's your family before you were born. Your great, great, great GrandParents, their parents, and their parents. All their brothers and sisters and cousins too. See what I mean? Those people are called your ancestors.

Sam: Yes. I see what you would mean. That would make me feel even sadder.

PaPa: Well, it's getting late and I gotta get up early tomorrow. So, we best call it a night. Take a little time to think about what it must have felt like to be a slave and what it would feel like if you found your ancestors were slaves.

Sam: I'd rather not, but I don't think I'll be able to think of much else. I sure hope I'll be able to stop thinking about it long enough to get some sleep tonight.

MaMa: I'm sure a cup of hot chocolate will help you get some sleep.

PaPa: Hot chocolate also helps when you get a backache!

MaMa: You think chocolate helps EVERYTHING.

PaPa: And your point is?

MaMa: I give up. You're nuts!! Good night PaPa. Good night Sam.

PaPa: Sleep tight, Sam. Give your PaPa a big hug!

Sam: m- m- m- m- m-m Good night PaPa.

PaPa: Good night.

Chapter 4

Sam: PaPa. Something's been bothering me.

PaPa: And what might that be, Sam?

Sam: I miss Mom and Dad. You told me when I got older, you'd tell me about them.

PaPa: It's a sad story. But I think you're old enough to hear it. Come sit by me. When you were just a teeny, tiny child, you and your mom and dad used to laugh and play a lot. And I mean a lot. Your mom and dad loved to take you on walks. Sometimes they'd take you out to swim and play. They'd read books to you and teach you how to read and write. Your mom taught you how to cook healthy food and take care of yourself. Your dad liked to help you build things and play pitch and catch with you. Y'all never got tired of each other. Wherever one was, the other would follow with a big smile. Then one day you were got really, fussy. This was very unusual for you. A few hours later, you got a high fever. The doctor said you needed medicine ASAP. But she didn't have any. So, your mom and dad hopped on their bikes and rode 75 miles to Quinville to get your medicine. They got there in less than a day. That was incredible. It had to be some kind of record. They were exhausted. They hurt worse than a centipede with sore feet. But still, they hurried home with your medicine. They were halfway back home when they realized they had both caught the same illness you had. They knew if they rode back to Quinville, you would not get your medicine on time. If they came straight home with your medicine, they would be unable to get medicine for themselves. They were in a pickle!

Sam: E-e-ewwwww! Yuck! But their ain't no way they could fit in a pickle. No way!!

PaPa: That's true. But the word pickle has another meaning. I said they were in a pickle. This is just another way of saying they were in a bad situation. And your Mom and Dad were definitely in a really, bad situation. So, they made up their mind and came straight home. They gave you your medicine and hugged you for the few hours they had left. They were so sad that they were seeing you for the last time. But they were ecstatic that you had a bunch of years left to live. MaMa and I made a promise to your mom and dad. We vowed to raise you as good as we could in these trying times. We knew it'd be tough. But raising you has been an extraordinary pleasure for us. And I promise, we miss your mom and dad as much as you do.

Sam: What did I have?

PaPa: You had something called Tetanus. When I was young, they'd give all the kids a special medicine called a vaccine. This would prevent them from catching Tetanus and spreading it. So, when I was young, nobody ever got Tetanus.

Sam: But people DO get Tetanus now. Why don't the doctors keep medicine on hand for emergencies?

PaPa: Back in the day, there were drug stores that would store more medicine than you can imagine. You could almost always get what you needed in an hour or so. But BLM raided more and more drug stores. Since so many businesses were being vandalized and burned to the ground, businesses were shutting down. People no longer had jobs and had no money to buy medicine. So, one by one the pharmaceutical companies had to shut down, like almost all the other companies. The drug stores that weren't burned to the ground salvaged what meds they could and hid them for emergencies. If you had gotten sick 10 years earlier, we could have gotten your medicine and your parent's medicine in less than an hour. You'd probably be having supper with your mom and dad right now. Or maybe fussing about how much homework you have.

Sam: I wish I could remember them better. It seems so long ago.

PaPa: It'll be our pleasure to refresh your memory whenever you want to think about your mom and dad. Me and MaMa miss your mom and dad very much. We think about them every single day.

MaMa: When we get home from school tomorrow, I will show you some pictures of your Mom and Dad. They're old and faded with cracks, but they will help you remember.

PaPa: It's past my bedtime. I think I'm gonna go to bed and dream about your mom and dad. Good night all.

MaMa: I think we're ALL gonna dream about your mom and dad. Good night!

Sam: I guess it's anonymous. Good night!

MaMa: I'm sure you mean unanimous. And you're right! Good night!

Chapter 5

PaPa: You 'bout ready for bed, Sam?

Sam: I sure am. I didn't get much sleep last night. I couldn't stop thinking 'bout how I'd feel if I was a slave. I feel so sorry for those slaves. That just isn't right. How could anyone own another person like you'd own a dog? Thinking 'bout that just makes me furious. I'd never let anyone own me.

PaPa: If it happened to you, you wouldn't have had much of a choice. You would just have a miserable life hoping, wishing, and praying you'd be a free person one day. It must've seemed like that would never happen. Some slaves ran away, but they usually got caught. Their owners often beat the heck out of 'em and punished 'em so badly the other slaves were too scared to even try to escape. It must've seemed truly hopeless.

PaPa: Unfortunately, slavery has been around for almost as long as mankind has existed.

Sam: But why?

PaPa: I'm certainly no expert, but I've done some reading on this and I have my personal opinions. I think for a long time, man was just like all the other animals in the world. They lived in the wild. And just like all the other wild animals, they just had two things on their To-Do list. The first thing they had to do was get food so they wouldn't starve to death. They were just like all the other animals, so they couldn't just go to a nearby farm to get food. They had to hunt for their own food or starve to death. The second thing they had to do was not become food. All the other animals had to look for food, too. So, if a lion or tiger or bear or something thought they could catch you – they'd try. And if they caught you - Voila! You've become a meal. Now, you don't have to worry about getting food anymore. Of course, that wouldn't be a good thing.

Sam: I didn't know we used to live like the animals.

PaPa: Well, that's what some people say. Other people have different ideas. We don't know of anyone who was around back then, so it's hard to know for sure. But, sometime, somehow, someway man found a way to plant crops and domesticate animals for food.

Sam: Huh?

PaPa: I know that's some big words for a little girl. All that means is that people didn't always have gardens full of potatoes and carrots and the like. They had to find berries and fruits and nuts in the forest. Sometimes, they had to travel far to find them. Same thing with meat. They had to go wherever they could to find animals to hunt for meat. Now, we keep the animals in fences until we need them for meat or milk. Humans have transformed themselves from hunters and gatherers to FARMERS.

Sam: I think I like being a farmer better.

PaPa: You better believe it. Now, people could create all the food they need. They could store some for winter and even have extra they could trade for other things they wanted.

Sam: Like what?

PaPa: Maybe spices to make the food taste better. Maybe clothing. Maybe firewood or medicine. Maybe even protection. I guess they'd trade for whatever they needed to survive and make life a little easier. I'm not really sure.

Sam: You mean you weren't there?

PaPa: Sam???!!! Are you suggesting that your PaPa is ancient?

Sam: I'm sorry, PaPa. It's just that you're so young for your looks.

PaPa: You're gonna get yours Sam. One day you'll get old like me.

Sam: Never.

PaPa: You'd better hope you get to be old like me. It's much better than the alternative. And it's really not too bad getting old, especially when you have a wonderful granddaughter like I have.

Sam: I prefer having a wonderful, old PaPa like I have!

PaPa: Come here, Sam. PaPa needs a big hug.

Sam: I just happen to have one. Um-m-m-m-m I'm tired. Can we go to sleep now?

MaMa: Would you happen to have another?

Sam: Hum! Let me see.

MaMa: Why don't you check while I make you and PaPa a cup of hot chocolate.

PaPa: Confucius say why have a cup of hot chocolate when you can have a cup of hot chocolate and chocolate chip cookies?

Sam: Who's Confucius?

MaMa: A very, old, and wise man?

Sam: You mean like PaPa?

PaPa: Exactly like PaPa! Except for the old part.

MaMa: Actually, I mean exactly like PaPa, except for the WISE part.

PaPa: MaMa! MaMa! You know I'm the youngest and wisest man in this house.

MaMa: PaPa! PaPa! You're the ONLY man in this house.

PaPa: MaMa! You're making me tired. After I empty my hot chocolate cup, I'm gonna hit the sack. Tomorrow we can talk about man's farms.

Sam: And woman's farms?

PaPa: Yup! When I say MAN'S farms, I really means man's and woman's. Sometimes, people use the word MAN to refer to MANKIND. When we talk about mankind, we mean humans. That can be men, women, children, black, white, yellow, red – ALL humans. It's just always been referred to as MANKIND – MAN for short. Maybe, a more meaningful word would be humankind, but it's been called mankind - or man - for so long, the word just stuck.

Sam: How do you know all this stuff, PaPa.

PaPa: KNOW is a very, big word. Very often, we hear this and that. We read this and that. And we kinda figure things out as best as we can based on what we already know (or what think we know). This is called reasoning. Sometimes we are right. Sometimes, well maybe not so right. So, it's more accurate to say "The way I see it….." than to say "I know!". As you get older, learn more stuff and you have more experiences, you'll change your mind about some of the things you say you KNOW. This is good because it shows that you are being open-minded.

Sam: This really doesn't make a whole lot of sense to me.

PaPa: Okay! Think of this. When you were just a kid. I told you the Earth was shaped like a sphere. Or should I say great bi-i-i-ig ball.".

Sam: I remember. I said "NO WAY! You're just teasing me. It's so easy to see the world is flat."

PaPa: And now????

Sam: Now I know the Earth is round.

PaPa: So, you KNEW the Earth was flat. Now, you KNOW the Earth is round. They can't both be true. So, that just confirms that just because we KNOW something, doesn't mean you are right. So, what lesson did you learn?

Sam: Keep an open mind because you may be wrong.

PaPa: Also, sometimes you can be right, but things will change. Today, you KNOW you can't light up your house by flipping a switch. But, one day we may get electricity again and if you continue saying you KNOW you can't light up your house by flipping a switch, you'd be wrong.

Sam: I see the light. You must've flipped a switch.

PaPa: Ha! Ha! Ha! You're such a jokester!

Sam: I wonder where I got that from? Seriously! I do understand and I will do my best to keep an open mind.

MaMa: Here y'all go! Hot chocolate for my open-minded family.

PaPa: Thanks for the hot chocolate.

Sam: Yeah! Thanks, MaMa. Good night!

PaPa: Good night, MaMa. Good night, Sam.

Chapter 6

Sam: PaPa. A few nights ago, you were telling me about slaves, then about farms. How in the world did you go from slaves to farms? What do farms have to do with slaves?

PaPa: Well Sam, farming was a huge step for mankind. But there's a problem. If you wanna run a farm, you need two things. First you need land. You can't grow crops without land.

Sam: Duh!

PaPa: To be a farmer you had to get some land and grow crops on it. You also had to protect the land. Other people might try to take your land from you. You also had to protect the farm from animals who wanted to eat your crop – or even eat you!

Sam: Yeow!!!

Papa: Yeow is right! So, you had 2 options. You could work longer and harder. But you still can produce only so much. Or you could get more people to help. But that wasn't cheap. So, how do you get more help? Back then, thousands and thousands of years ago, the way you got land was to have a war until the people who lived on the land you wanted left.

Sam: What if they didn't leave?

PaPa: I dread saying this! But if they wouldn't leave – you'd kill 'em. I know! I know! That sounds harsh, but that's just how war worked back then. If you don't kill them, they'd kill you. I'm sure you've heard the saying, "War is Hell!" Well, that's an understatement. War is worse than hell. Someone somewhere must have thought, "Hey, man! Instead of killing these guys, let's make them work for us. That worked out great – for the farmers anyway. Later, some businessman somewhere must've figured, "Hey, I can make money selling slaves!" So, he decided, "I know how I can make some extra money. I'll go to another country where people can't protect themselves. I'll catch me some slaves and sell'em to farmers who need help. It's good for the farmers because they don't have to go out to get slaves and it's good for me because I make a profit." Hence, selling people to people became a profitable business benefitting everyone, except the slaves of course. The slaves lost their freedom, their dignity, their culture, their families and often their lives.

Sam: O-o-o-oh, PaPa. That is just so sad!

PaPa: Sam, this is probably the saddest turn of events in all of history. And it happened so early we can't even tell when. We just know that most civilizations at that time had slaves and slave owners for century after century after century. It's kind of hard to call that civilization. Nevertheless, everyone did it and no one had a problem with it – except the slaves of course. Slaves worked the fields, built buildings, tended to the owners and whatever else needed to be done. They had little hope of ever having a free life and raising a family. Well, they could raise a family, but their children became slaves, too. Who wants that for their kids? Slavery had become as common and accepted as raising livestock for food. By today's standards, you can't get much more immoral. But by yesteryear's standards, it was brutal, but considered a perfectly legitimate necessity.

Sam: But that's just wrong.

PaPa: I know! I know! That's hard to understand. Think of it this way. There are places in the world today where people eat dogs. To us, that is absolutely disgusting. But, does that make it wrong? There are other places where it is illegal to eat pigs and they think that is unthinkable. Does that make it wrong for us have bacon for breakfast? Something may change one day, and we'll look back and say, "UUUHHHGGGHHH! We actually used to eat pigs! OH, YUCKY, YUCKY." It's hard to resolve who's right and who's wrong. Maybe, no one is really right and no one is really wrong. Maybe we are just different. We have to analyze our traditions and see WHY we have different values and behaviors. But somehow, someway we've got to find a way to live together in peace.

Sam: So, why don't we still have slaves today?

PaPa: Sam! I'm ashamed of you! I taught you better than that! Why would you want to have slaves today?

Sam: I definitely would NOT want to have slaves today. I just don't understand. You said everyone thought slavery was acceptable. What changed? Why don't we still find it acceptable?

PaPa: I think that's the wrong question. The right question would be, why did people think slavery was acceptable back then. Morality is one's sense of right and wrong. Perhaps the best way to judge if something is right or wrong is to put yourself in their shoes. That's called empathy. In the case of slavery, would slavery be fine if YOU were the slave?

Sam: NO! NO! NO! NO!

PaPa: Very good! I think every sane person would agree. The question is, why did people think it was acceptable thousands of years ago? Maybe, it was because they felt their very existence depended on it. It's like survival was more important than morality. I guess I really can't answer that question. I can only ponder. What do you think?

Sam: I think they could have found another way to survive. Without slaves!!!

PaPa: Questions! Questions! And more questions. You're gonna wear my brain out. But, please don't ever stop asking questions. That's how we grow. I want your favorite question in the whole wide world to be, "WHY?".

Sam: But WHY?

PaPa: YES! YES! YES! GREAT START! Keep asking "Why?". Don't ever stop. If everyone would ask questions before getting into a fight, there would be a whole lot less fighting. So, I want "WHY?" to be your favorite question. Ask it often. And this is especially important – **ask it of yourself**. You should have a reason for the things you do. That reason may be simply because you enjoy it or because everyone else does it. But there is a reason. So, ask yourself "WHY?" You'll probably find you have good reasons for most of the things you do. Some things, maybe not such good reasons. I don't mean you have bad reasons. Maybe, you just don't know why.

PaPa: I'm kinda tired, but I promise tomorrow night, I'll tell you about the men from England who voyaged to a new world.

Sam: A new world? I thought we only had one world!

PaPa: I'm gonna have to postpone that until tomorrow night. My brain is fried.

Sam: My brain is tired, too. I'm gonna have to sleep on it.

MaMa: I had to sneak in and get a good night hug!

PaPa: Here you go! M-m-m-m-m!

MaMa: Not you, PaPa! **Sam!!!!**

Sam: M-m-m-m-m! Good night, MaMa.
Good night, PaPa.

MaMa: Good night, Sam.
Good night, PaPa.

PaPa: Good night, Sam.
Good night, MaMa

Sam: I love you MaMa. Good night.

MaMa: Good night, Sam! I love you too.

Sam: Good night, PaPa.

PaPa: Good night, sweetheart.
Good night, John Boy.

Sam: Who's John Boy?

MaMa: Don't worry about John Boy! Yo crazy PaPa is just reminiscing about the old days. Good night, Sue Ellen.

Sam: I won't even ask!

Chapter 7

Sam: I can't wait PaPa. I'm so excited! You promised you'd tell me about a new world.

PaPa: I'm glad you're so excited. I won't keep you waiting another minute. You see, hundreds of years ago, everybody lived in Europe, Asia, or Africa. Or at least that's what everybody thought. They knew there was an ocean between Europe and Asia and that if they could sail across the ocean instead of traveling by land, it would save lots of time and money. Eventually, a ship sailed around the from Europe all the way around the world to Asia. Or so they thought. They thought they reached Asia. But actually, they reached a whole new world. A world no one in Europe even knew existed. It eventually became known as America. Yes, the America we live in today. No one even knew about it yet back them. That was hundreds of years ago.

Sam: That's strange that no one knew about it when we were living here.

PaPa: Back then, we weren't living here. Only the Native American's lived here. But the ship was so sure they had gone all around the world and landed in India, they called the people living there Indians.

Sam: That's funny!

PaPa: It may be funny, but the name Indians stuck until this very day. As time passed, more people from Europe moved to America to get away from their country. They wanted out for several reasons. For one thing, they wanted to practice religion however they wanted without the government interfering.

Sam: Why would the government care where you go to church?

PaPa Because the government WAS the church. Back then, most governments and churches were tied together. They were one and the same. But in this "New World" there were these 13 colonies. Each colony wanted to practice religion in their own way, but they were part of Europe, so they still had to follow England's religion. I think it was called the Church of England. So, when the America's founding fathers created the government, they intentionally left out religion. This was eventually referred to as the Wall of Separation Between Church and State.

Sam, I love you PaPa! I love it when you tell me these stories. It's like an adventure.

PaPa Well hold on to your seat because here comes the crazy part. The settlers in the new world started growing tobacco, sugarcane, and cotton. But they had a problem. They didn't have enough settlers to work the fields. Of course, there were slave traders more than willing to help. Over the course of a hundred years or so, the US imported thousands and thousands of slaves. Then the 13 colonies decided to break away from England and be their own country. They wanted to be free from England. Free from England's high taxation without representation. And free to practice whatever religion they wanted. So, the settlers broke away from England and eventually wrote the United Sates Constitution. The US Constitution was a document that formalized what America stood for and how it would work. Part of the constitution proclaims that it is the government's job to "Secure the Blessings of Liberty to Ourselves and Our Posterity." Our forefathers must've really struggled with this because some of them owned slaves. What a conundrum!

Sam: What a what?

PaPa: What a CONUNDRUM! That means what a confusing problem! Our forefathers believed all men should be free because freedom is a blessing of liberty. At the same time, they must've thought, "Oh, wow! If we're supposed to secure the blessings of liberty, we should secure them for everyone – and this includes our slaves. They have as much right to be free as anyone. But how can we run our businesses without slaves? We NEED our slaves!" How could our forefathers claim that part of their Constitution is to secure the Blessing of Liberty while they themselves owned slaves?

Sam: That seems backwards.

PaPa I've heard that our forefathers wanted to abolish slavery from day one. But two of the southern states said, "No Way Jose!". But our forefathers thought that it would be better to create the new nation and work on abolishing slavery later than to not create the new nation at all and just allow slavery to continue.

Sam: That sounds logical to me. I guess.

PaPa Me, too. Especially since at that time slavery was considered just another part of life. If something has been considered normal for thousands of years, it'll take time to change people's minds. Maybe hundreds of years later, people will wonder how they could have ever thought that was okay in the first place.

Sam: Well, it's good that one day, the new world decided to stop slavery.

PaPa Yes, that was a good thing. But it wasn't easy. You see, lots of people in the northern states made a living in factories. Many of the factories processed cotton with cotton gins. Most people in the southern states made a living by providing that cotton to the northern factories. And the only way to pick the cotton was with manual labor. And most of that labor was slave labor. So, the North did not rely on slavery like the South did and thought it should be abolished. Almost half the people in the south were slaves. The north and the south could never agree. Eventually, the south said they no longer wanted to be part of the United States and they became their own country named the Confederate States of America. But the north said "Oh, no you don't! You're still part of the United States". Since the North and the South couldn't agree, the bloodiest war in America began. The Civil War. More than half a million people died in the Civil War. The North won and the blacks were finally free – at least officially. But their problems were nowhere near over.

Sam: What do you mean, PaPa? They were FREE!

PaPa: The blacks were freed. Yes! But most of them couldn't read or write. They had no money to buy property. Businesses didn't want to hire them just because they were black. A lot of white people terrorized them just because they were black. A lot of white people probably thought of black people as inferior. They didn't want to eat in the same room, ride on the same bus, or even go to the same school. I think white people tried to think of slaves as less than human to condone having had them as slaves and treating them like animals.

Sam: My goodness. Do the blacks ever get a break?

PaPa For another 100 years, blacks were playing catch up. But they weren't having much luck. Finally, the government enacted laws to prevent discrimination and laws to help those who had been discriminated against to help them catch up.

Sam: Did it work?

PaPa No! Some of the laws actually made it worse for black people. I'm guessing this was not by accident. But at least it was a start. The wheels of change were in motion. Eventually, the blacks could go to the same schools as whites. They could eat in the same restaurants. Use the same restrooms. But there was still a lot of discrimination. Most of it was behind closed doors. That is, they were concealed and hard to prove. The amount of discrimination decreased, but at a snail's pace and it never disappeared completely. Not to this very day. It was like watching paint not dry. And the blacks didn't always treat the whites very nicely. This is completely understandable. They were just doing unto others as they had been done unto. So, some of the whites started treating the blacks worse, which made the blacks despise the whites more. So, they treated the whites worse which made the whites distrust the blacks which ended up in a continuous circle of discrimination, resentment, mistrust, misunderstanding and crude interactions. Eventually, some of the whites and some of the blacks came around. Relations were getting better, but only painstakingly slow.

Sam: I'm glad I wasn't a black person back then.

PaPa That wouldn't have been fun. It was a very confusing time. Slavery was just a part of life for so long – but who's fault was that? There were black slaves and white slaves. There were white slave owners and black slave owners. To slave owners, owning slaves became a matter of mere economics. After thousands of years of this atrocity, some white countries realized and admitted that slavery was undeniably wrong. So they ABOLISHED it. You wanna hear something really strange?

Sam: Yup!

PaPa: The first few countries to make slavery illegal were primarily white countries. But, it is white people who are typically saddled with the transgression of slavery. The United States was one of the first countries to abolish slavery. Now, the slaves were freed. But opinions and prejudices didn't change overnight. Convincing people that the practice of slavery they had known all their life was immoral was like convincing them that the sun doesn't revolve around the Earth! The slaves were free now. But they weren't prepared for the world they had been brought into. They weren't prepared for the menacing racism and terrorism they were about to face. And unprepared for the long uphill battle they would have to fight. No! Fun would not be the right word for their future. But they persevered with tenacity. While most of them struggled, a few made a decent living. Some moved up and were quite successful. Yet others had tremendous success as business owners, athletes, politicians and even President of the United States of America. And with their success, they fought racism. More and more blacks lived better lives and racism steadily declined. But as with everything – there were still a few bad apples.

MaMa: The fire was still lingering, so I made some hot chocolate.

PaPa: Confucius say, "She who makes hot chocolate deserves warm hug".

Sam: Sam says so, too! Come here, MaMa! U-u-u-m!

MaMa: Good night! I just finished my chores and I'm going to bed. Good night.

Sam: PaPa, what do you mean, "There were still a few bad apples!"

PaPa: It seems there are always a few bad apples. But it's late and that will have to wait for another night. Good night, Sam.

Sam: No! No! Not yet. I can tell by your voice, a few bad apples is going to be huge.

PaPa: Yes! Incredibly huge. But I had a long hard day. So, it will have to wait for another night.

Sam: Now you got me all wired up with curiosity. Good night PaPa.

PaPa: Good night, Sam.

Chapter 8

PaPa: Well, you've heard the old saying – One bad apple doesn't spoil the whole bunch.

Sam: PaPa, apples don't come in bunches. Bananas do.

PaPa: You are absolutely, correct. That's how we know one bad apple doesn't really spoil the whole bunch. But there are those that may disagree. America was in a time of unrest. Many believed racism was systemic and in epic proportions.

Sam: Say what?!

PaPa: Sorry 'bout the fancy words. Systemic means many believed that racism was built into the system. Kinda like there were laws to keep blacks oppressed. Epic just means there was a whole bunch of it. People started to voice their opinions. Blacks started protesting. Occasionally, some white people empathized with the blacks and joined the protest. Citizens spoke up as well as politicians. There were quite a few adults who tried to be friends with the blacks – and were often successful. The children didn't have to try very, hard. Most of them just did it naturally. That is, if their family and friends didn't influence them badly. You know, some people even wrote songs to promote racial equality. Would you like me to sing one for you?

Sam: Yes, PaPa. Please! Please!

MaMa: Don't let PaPa sing to you this soon after supper. I don't want to clean up a mess.

PaPa: I can take a hint. "Ebony and Ivory" will have to wait until your food goes down. May I continue?

Sam: Yup! Go right ahead, PaPa.

PaPa: The racial divide was narrowing. But there still were a few bad apples. And when those apples were bad, the media publicized it because the public wanted to see the sensational – not the ordinary. So, while the police across America were having millions of public contacts each day – there were some episodes of police behaving inappropriately. Of course, the media showed the one or two bad cases and completely ignored the multitude of good contacts completely. So, the blacks felt like the entire police force was sinister and targeting them for no reason. The whites see all blacks as criminals who don't follow the cop's instructions.

Sam: Can't get no worse than that!

PaPa: Wanna Bet!

PaPa: We'll get into the really bad stuff in a minute. But first, I mentioned a while back that there was a lot of confusion and misinformation. But why? I think because many American's lost the art of discussing issues face-to-face. They would hear things on the street and see things on the internet. They would assume it was all true and seldom take the time to research what was real and what was conjured. And when people had disagreements – they would often shout at each other and interrupt each other. It's almost impossible to resolve anything like that.

Sam: So how do we fix that?

PaPa: First off. We must be brave enough to face our friends and family when we think they're doing something wrong. Sometimes it's hard to disagree with them. But if you don't level with them, they'll probably assume you agree with them. Think about it. Someone had to have the guts to face their friends and family and say, "Hey! I really think slavery is just flat out wrong. How'd you like it if YOU were a slave?"

Sam: Why would that be hard?

PaPa: It's easy NOW because just about everyone agrees that slavery is absurdly wrong. Back then It would've been hard because slavery was just a way of life. It's like if you moved to a new town and found out they ate dogs for lunch. You knew they'd been eating dogs since the day they were born. So, they'd think you were nuts for saying eating dogs is wrong. So, you'd have to debate with them and discuss why you shouldn't eat dogs. And you must be ready to accept that you may not be able to convince them and you can't go ballistic if they don't agree. Sometimes it takes a long time to change people's mindset. Sometimes you may find THEY are right and you gotta change your mindset. There's nothing wrong with that. That's how we evolve.

Sam: You said we have to DEBATE with them. Is that like wrestling with them?

PaPa: No! No! No! Not at all! Let's talk about debating. I'm not a debater, but I'd like to share with you a few ways to DISCUSS things in a civilized manner. First, here are what I call Rules of Engagement. I wish this were a book so I could just put them in an appendix! But this handwritten copy will have to do because we no longer have copy machines. (*See the Rules of Engagement at the end of the book.*)

Sam: I read 'em PaPa. Sounds pretty simple.

PaPa: Okay. This is how it works. First there is a proposition. That is a claim that someone makes. The debate is to convince others that the proposition is either true or false. Tomorrow night the proposition will be: We should not raise cows to eat. Sam, I know you don't like us killing cows so you will argue that the proposition is true. MaMa will argue that the proposition is false. Sam, I'll give you a chance to give your view WITH NO

INTERUPTIONS. Then MaMa will give her view WITH NO INTERRUPTIONS. Then MaMa will comment on your view with no interruptions. Then you will comment on MaMa's view with no interruptions. They I'll give y'all each a chance to ask each other questions. And when you answer the questions, there will be no interruptions. If this were a formal debate, we could let an audience ask questions then vote to see who wins. But this is not going to be formal at all.

Sam: Sounds good to me.

PaPa: Oh, wait! Wait! Did I mention there will be NO INTERRUPTIONS!

Sam: Only about a bazillion times.

PaPa: Okay! Get some sleep and think about your arguments for tomorrow. How are you going to convince us that we should not raise cows to eat. Good night, Sam.

Sam: No problem. This'll be so-o-o easy, I won't even have to think much about it.

PaPa: Don't be so sure. Now get some rest.

Sam: Good night, PaPa.

PaPa: Good night, Sam.

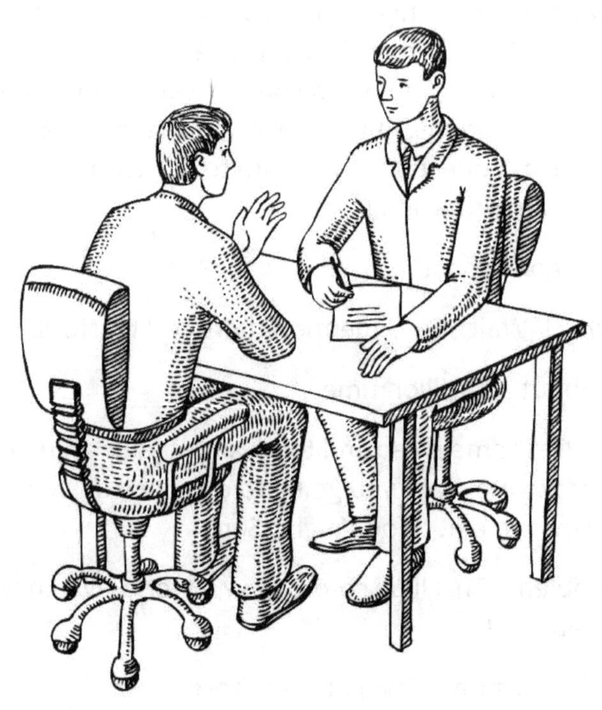

Chapter 9

PaPa: Goo-oo-oo-oo-ood evening ladies. Tonight's the night you've been waiting for. It's DEBATE TIME! The proposition for tonight's debate is: We should not raise cows to eat. In this corner in favor of the proposition is Sam. She will be debating that we should not raise cattle to eat. In that corner in opposition of the proposition is MaMa. She will be debating that we need to raise cattle to eat. We will begin with opening arguments. We'll start with the proponent of the proposition. Sam, you have the spotlight.

Sam: I say we should not raise cattle to eat. They should have their freedom and be able to roam and enjoy the outdoors with their calves. It is also cruel that we shoot them in the head to kill them before we eat them. I say we let them all go free to live their lives in peace.

PaPa: Thank you, Sam. Good job! MaMa, you have the spotlight.

MaMa: Thank you, PaPa. I say we SHOULD raise cattle to eat. Some animals eat grass for food. Some eat meat. We eat both to survive.

Sam: We could live on

PaPa: ORDER! ORDER! Sam you are out of order. You need to give MaMa a chance to give her side of the argument just like she gave you yours. Remember, NO INTERRUPTIONS.

Sam: OK! Sorry.

MaMa: Continuing. We need their meat to eat and in return we feed them and care for them. They will probably live longer on the farm than they would in the wild. I think that is a fair compromise.

PaPa: Sam, you get to comment on what MaMa said.

Sam: I disagree that we need meat to survive. We could just eat more bread and fish.

PaPa: MaMa. Do you wish to comment on Sam's position?

MaMa: Sam suggested that we should give the cow's their freedom to roam and live their own lives in peace. I would argue that cattle in the wild would not live in peace. In the wild, they must constantly look for food. More than half of them will become a meal before they reach adulthood. We offer cattle a constant supply of food and care for them for years before we eat them. We also take care of their young and protect them. And they are much less likely to become wolf chow in our care than if they were roaming the hillside. And I promise, we shoot them in the head to kill them because it is a much more humane death than they would experience in the wild. Wolves and cats eat animals while they are still alive. Let me describe that to you. First, one wolf may

Sam: Stop! Stop! Stop! MaMa, you convinced me. You convinced me. If I had to choose between being a cow in the wild or a cow on a farm, I'd be a cow on a farm any day. I can't think of anything worse than being eaten alive.

PaPa: Great debate. Normally, we'd ask each other a few questions. But that will not be necessary today. Thank y'all both for participating. I'm glad that Sam is now convinced that raising cows to eat is a good thing. I'm even happier that we were able to have a nice, respectful debate. Most discussions will be even less formal than this. I hope this little exercise will help you settle disputes politely in the future.

Sam: That was actually kinda fun. I'm so glad MaMa didn't describe cows being eaten alive.

PaPa: Yup! I agree. Thanks, MaMa. Next time you have a dispute with someone, try to use some of these techniques. Respect your opponent and hopefully they will respect you right back. Feel free to write down these Rules of Engagement for them so y'all will be playing by the same rules. It sounds easy, but old habits are hard to break. Just keep working at it.

Sam: Will do. I'm beat, so I think I'll hit the sack. Good night, MaMa. Good night, PaPa.

PaPa: Good night, Sadie. I'm gonna hit the sack too.

MaMa: Good night Sadie. I'll see you in the morning.

Chapter 10

PaPa: Sam, we were talking about how white people thought black people were bad and black people thought white people were bad. You thought things couldn't get worse and I hinted that they did get much worse. Here's why. America had entered a time when citizens were obsessed with civil rights. Then it erupted like a volcano. Citizens demanded their rights be honored.

Sam: What's wrong with that? We SHOULD honor their rights!

PaPa: Yes! But one thing you absolutely can't forget. You rights end the minute they impose on someone else's rights. For example, it has been said "The right to swing your fist ends where another man's nose begins."

Sam: That is an excellent point. It's true. So true!

PaPa: Yes, but then the fun began. There were a small number of people started making claims and making up rights that were absolutely, absurd. Men claimed to be women. Women claimed to be men. Some people even claimed to be animals – like dogs or cats.

Sam: That's sounds crazy.

PaPa: The problem wasn't that they were making these claims. Anyone can think whatever they want and claim they are right. The problem was that they were offended when you didn't agree with them. And they believed they had the RIGHT to not be offended. This completely contradicted free speech because someone will be offended by just about anything you say. Some blacks claimed they had the right to be compensated for being underprivileged as a black person. Some citizens objected to historical monuments that honored historical figures who owned slaves. This became a problem when the citizens took it upon themselves to destroy the monuments. Some citizens objected to the United States protecting itself by guarding its borders. They claimed that this is the land of the free and that anyone has the right to just walk in and live here. For some reason they didn't think we should protect ourselves from terrorists! Then, an organization named Black Lives Matter was formed under the premise that white cops were killing black men, needlessly.

Sam: That's a bad thing. Why would cops kill anyone needlessly?

PaPa: Well, Sam. This is where things really get confusing. Remember, back then there was so much communication going on that it was hard to tell what was real and what was fake. So, at any given moment, you could look at the news and see white cops killing black people, black people committing crimes, black criminals threatening cops and resisting arrest, black people saying white people were privileged, white people saying that just wasn't so, white people saying black people were bad, white people saying blacks were getting handouts from the government just because they were black. So, it was really, hard to tell what was actually going on. Then, IT HAPPENED!

Sam: What happened?

PaPa: IT happened. Pictures of white cops killing black people hit the news and BLM went ballistic.

Sam: Why were the cops killing black people?

PaPa: Go-o-o-o-od question. These pictures didn't tell the whole story and lots of people didn't care to find out. BLM started taking over cities. They'd crowd streets to block traffic. They'd bully people who didn't agree with them. They'd break windows and burn cars and buildings. They'd break in and loot businesses and beat up people who resisted them. They'd take over police stations, overpower police with rocks and glass. They claimed that cops who protected themselves and the community were using excessive force. This put cops in a no-win situation.

Sam: But the cops were just trying to help.

PaPa: Yes, but according to BLM, any help the cops delivered, was an act against BLM and therefore racially motivated. It seemed like BLM was trying to get rid of the cops.

Sam: This makes no sense. Why would you get rid of the people who are there to protect you?

PaPa: Again – we were in a very nebulous time. I can only tell you what it seemed like to me. And remember, like everyone else, I had very, limited information. BLM claimed they were causing all this chaos because white cops were killing black people. But, lots of people questioned what black lives was really all about.
-- Many people asked, "If black lives really mattered, why did black people kill so many black people?" Black people killed many more black people than white cops did.
-- Many people thought it was a great cause, but that the message got lost in the violence.
-- Many people thought racism was so bad, they condoned BLM's actions.
-- Many people thought cops were targeting more blacks because more black people were committing crimes.
-- Many people thought more blacks were getting killed because more blacks were resisting arrest.
-- Many people thought it wrong for people who have never been slaves to blame slavery on people who have never owned slaves.
-- Many people, especially cops, must have wondered, "If the cops let a criminal resisting arrest flee and the criminal harms someone else, would the cop be held liable?"

Sam: That is so confusing. How can you decide what to do when you have bad information?

PaPa: I'm not sure that anyone ever answered that question. But when things got really bad, we assumed some of the stories we were hearing had to be true.

PaPa: It's hard to imagine, but it gets even worse. Government officials couldn't agree with each other, so they were fighting amongst themselves more than they were governing. There were those government officials who took sides with BLM and condoned their lawlessness. So, the vandalism and city takeovers were left unchecked and expanded like your belly on Thanksgiving Day!

Sam: You mean like YOUR belly on Thanksgiving.

PaPa: Ouch! Ya got me. Anyway. Things got so bad, people and businesses couldn't live with the vandalism and terrorism anymore. So, slowly they began leaving the cities being taken over. There weren't enough people left in the cities to rent homes and offices, or go to restaurants, bars, and movies. So, more business closed, and more people left. Now, you have less people, so you have less taxes being paid, so cities don't have enough money to maintain themselves. So, taxes went up which caused more people to leave. It was a vicious spiral that didn't last long. It couldn't last long. Thriving metropolitan areas became ghost towns or crime infested free-for-alls. Tons of people were out of work and the government didn't have enough money to help them. Welfare was all but stopped because governments weren't collecting enough taxes. People went hungry and there was little if any help for people who got sick. Many died. The good life as we knew it was gone. Maybe forever.

Sam: Why didn't everyone raise a big stink and say "Stop! This is wrong! Something has to change!"

PaPa: Perhaps one of the worst things that we lost was our freedom of speech. Yes, the Constitution said we had Freedom of Speech. But if you disagreed with people of differing opinions, you were labelled a racist or something like that and there were no cops to protect you against retaliation. So, people kept their mouths shut. They kept their opinions to themselves. And without free speech, ideas which lead to positive change are suppressed. So, we ended up where we are now. Now, everyone has to fend for themselves. We live in villages for protection trying not to become extinct. We have almost no hospitals, doctors, or prescription drugs. We are in a struggle for our very survival. Many have lost the struggle. Many of our friends and entire families are lost forever. And for what? Now, people are surviving in small villages like this. We specialize in making ammo for protection. McDonaldville specializes in growing food. Smithville specializes in raising livestock. Quinville specializes in healthcare and medicine. Jonestown specializes in building huts and infrastructure. We all barter our goods and services with each other to survive. We try to have larger families now to keep our population growing because there is strength in numbers. Smaller families, especially families missing a mommy or daddy, were the hardest hit because now we have to do so much more just to survive. So, part of what we do is to help others in the community who need a helping hand. We all need a hand once in a while and it's up to us to provide it. The government used to do this, but we have not progressed that far. I know this is the only life you have ever known. More than half of our children die before they get to be teenagers. We die when we get infections because we don't have enough medicine. Our travel is limited, so we can't travel to get medicine and see a doctor. Without running water and electricity, food spoilage and sanitation is a major problem. There are so-o-o many things we took for granted back them! I really wish life could have been better for you. I never imagined the world would come to this. I don't think anyone did.

Sam: PaPa! Do you miss the old life?

PaPa: Yes! And NO! I miss taking food for granted. Being able to drive a few miles to a store and buy as much meat, milk and vegetables as you wanted. I really miss junk food.

Sam: Junk food? YUCK! That's disgusting.

MaMa: Yo PaPa would have lived on junk food if he could have. Junk food is basically sugar and preservatives in a wrapper.

Sam: If PaPa ate so many preservatives, why does he still look so old.

MaMa: I like that question! Preservatives were stuff you added to food to keep it from spoiling. Sometimes, someone would fix some food and store it in a can. Then someone would ship a bunch of cans to the store. Then you'd buy it from the store. You could keep this food in a pantry for months or even years before it would go bad.

Sam: O-o-o-h-h! I like that. That's so much better than our beans rotting in a couple of weeks.

MaMa: And PaPa's favorite, junk food, was called junk food because it was very unhealthy. What's really bad is that junk food tasted good. And eating junk food made you want to eat more junk food. PaPa was not just a chocoholic. He was a first class junk food junky. Good, Lord have pity on him. If junk food were available today, PaPa would probably cause a world-wide junk food shortage. Shame on you PaPa!

PaPa: Guilty as charged! Getting back on course, I miss hot showers and long lazy weekends eating junk food and listening to oldies.

Sam: What an oldie?

PaPa: Oldies is old music. It's music I grew up with. Back then there were groups that would get together just to make music. They made music about everything. They made songs about love, hate, living, dying, racism, religion, cars, beaches, food, girls, boys, dogs, even unicorns. You name it - someone probably wrote a song about it. I never got tired of listening to the oldies. Oldies bring back priceless memories. Even now, when I can barely hear, those old songs live on in my mind like they did when I was young. Would you like me to sing one to you?

Sam: I'll pass. MaMa told me you won 2nd place in a singing competition once. She said you lost to a frog with laryngitis and that y'all were the only two in the contest.

PaPa: And when did she tell you this.

Sam: When she was explaining how smart you are.

PaPa: Just how smart did she say I was?

Sam: Smarter than a rock.

PaPa: She said that, huh?

Sam: Well, she said you were smarter than the average rock.

PaPa: Well, she's not so smart either. Look who she married.

Sam: I'd say that makes MaMa pretty darned smart.

PaPa: You couldn't be more correct little girl.

Sam: I bet you wish it could be like the old days again, huh?

PaPa: Don't get me wrong, the old days were nice. But now I realize there was a downside. People started spending too much time on their phone and computer. They didn't spend much time talking face-to-face like we are now. There is no part of my day that I value more than the time we spend having our evening chats. If going back to living like the old days meant not having our chats – FORGET IT! You and the time we spend together mean more than all the old day's conveniences combined.

Sam: I love you too, PaPa.

PaPa: You know, time doesn't stand still. In the past few years, we've advanced quite a bit. We were single families struggling to survive. Now, families have gathered to form communities. We work together for the good of the entire community. And while we've been growing, there is a group of elders who have been organizing a movement. They want to get the United States back to being a real country again.

Sam: That sounds great!

PaPa: The trouble is many of us forgot what it means to be an American. Some never really knew in the first place. These elders wrote a Declaration of an American Patriot. This is like a pact affirming values we should embrace and behaviors we should strive for if we are to pull the United States together. The elders are hoping to get as many people as possible to sign so we can get back to being the United States of America again. Anyone can stop by the meeting hut to sign. We have until the end of the month to sign.

Sam: I'll sign! I'll sign!

PaPa: Not so fast! This isn't something you just sign! Here. I've got a copy for you. It's only 2 pages, but it's a pretty, tough read. If this chat were in a book, I'd stick this in as an appendix. But since we don't have copy machines anymore, I hand wrote you your very own copy. The Declaration of an American Patriot was intentionally written in a similar style to Thomas Jefferson's Declaration of Independence. That's the document used to announce our separation from England over 200 years ago. I'd like you to read this – the Declaration of an American Patriot. Every word of it! Really think about what each word means and decide if you really want to be an American Patriot. If you do, we'll talk to as many people as we can and see if they want to join the band wagon.

In the old days, we'd just post this Declaration on the internet so the whole world could sign it. We'd tell everybody, "Hey! I saw something you might be interested in. Check out https://www.change.org/DeclarationOfAnAmericanPatriot and read the new declaration. If it is something you're interested in, please sign. Maybe, just maybe, if we can get more and more people to sign, we can get more and more people to start talking about it. Seems like half the people alive today weren't even alive when America was at its peak. Maybe we can all get together and make America even greater than it was before."

But this is NOW, not yesteryear. So, let's talk to everyone we know. Let's ask them if they are interested in signing and committing to helping reconstitute what was once the greatest country in the world, The United States of America.

The End!

And the Beginning!

What happens next is up to all of us!

How to sign the Declaration of an American Patriot

Today, signing the Declaration of an American Patriot is about as easy as can be. Just go to https://www.change.org/DeclarationOfAnAmericanPatriot .

The entire document is less than 800 words. But it's really a lot to think about. The document is not perfect. But what is? Please read! If you agree with the Declaration of an American Patriot – would you scroll back up to the top of the page and please sign. More importantly, pass it on. Pass it on to someone near, someone far, someone old, someone young, someone you think agrees with the declaration and someone you think won't agree. Let's get the conversation started.

Mysterious Narrating Voice

Narrated with my best vocal impersonation of James Earl Jones

And so, it began, just like in 1776. In 1776, English settlers signed the Declaration of Independence declaring that they were divorcing themselves from England. Now, American survivors are distancing themselves from organizations that act more like terrorists than Americans. A country plagued by narcissism and social justice extremists is now being reclaimed by patriots striving to revive their country, making it a more perfect union that secures its citizens blessings of liberty. Have the protestors learned that violence is self-defeating? Has the silent majority learned to speak up? Have the elders learned not to appease to the mob just to get their votes? Is this the resurgence that will make America great again? Have we learned our lesson? Or is this but one more iteration of a cycle doomed to be repeated over and over and over again like the inevitable sunrise and sunsets which fill our existence. Time will tell. American's will decide.

What do you think?

Make a difference!

Pass it on!

Rules of Engagement

1. Do not interrupt when someone else is speaking.
2. Avoid raising your voice.
3. No name calling.
4. Stay on task. Don't get off topic by using poor analogies.
5. Avoid using words like STUPID or DUMB. Use more descriptive words like ineffective, inappropriate, irrational, not cost effective. It's hard to defend a statement that says something is stupid. But it is much easier to defend a statement with a more descriptive word.
6. Avoid using the words ALWAYS and NEVER. Very few things are ALWAYS or NEVER, and your opposition can use a valid example to show your ALWAYS or NEVER argument to be illogical.
7. Remember, your opposition believes they are correct just as much as you believe you are. Respect their opinion even though you don't agree with it like you'd want them to respect yours.
8. Take responsibilities for you actions and words. Don't push the blame on someone or something else. Be proud to admit when you were wrong and were open minded enough to change your mind.

Declaration of an American Patriot

When in the course of a countries lifetime, it becomes necessary for law abiding citizens to openly, aggressively, and legally oppose movements which distort, abuse and oppose the law to promote their evil, misguided agenda and inflict their obstinate actions and deplorable virtues upon us and lead us away from our forefathers noble vision.

Our courageous and determined forefathers, however imperfect, held these truths to be self-evident, that all men are created equal, that they are endowed by their Creator with certain unalienable rights, that among these are life, liberty and the pursuit of happiness. Though we have never completely fulfilled these ends, whenever any movement becomes destructive of progress towards these ends, it is not just the right of the people to abolish such a destructive movement, but the obligation of the people.

We too must cling firmly to these truths if we are to honor the legacy bestowed upon us by or forefathers and nurture that legacy for posterity. But when a movement to secure these rights, either by conceit, narcissism, or misinformation, overtake the very rights that have been so valiantly fought for in the past and in the present, decline is imminent. Empathy and compassion, indeed, will dictate that such movements should not be abolished for light and brief causes. But patience has run out, tolerances exceeded, and absurdities inundate. To allow this to continue is irrational as the imminence of permanence is on America's threshold. This could be no more evident than by the abundance of free speech suppressed, mobs condoned, crime spikes, homes destroyed, businesses destroyed, livelihoods lost and even life itself terminated.

We are observing detrimental trends in our lifetime:

- Public institutions suppressing our freedom of speech.
- Citizens insisting, they have the right to not be offended.
- Citizens considering criticism offensive and unspeakable.

- Political Correctness trumping truth.
- Our forefathers of yesteryear being held accountable by today's standards.
- "Innocent until proven guilty" becoming history.
- No justice No Peace, Aka CHAOS, becoming unopposed and acceptable.
- Decline of patriotism.
- Decline of appreciation for being an American.

As Americans, we direly need to revitalize our aspirations and responsibilities. We must:

- Preserve and embrace our history. The good as a reminder of what we stand for and the evil as a reminder of what we have overcome.
- Magnify adherence to our forefathers founding ideals. But do not expect total change overnight or even in the brevity of a lifetime that which has been universally accepted for all time. Patience is indeed a virtue. Embrace all progress achieved.
- Judge not our irreplaceable, foundational forefathers and historical figures by today's standards, nor think of them as Gods.
- Ask not what our country can do for us, but what we can do for your country.
- Embrace American values.
- Participate in government and vote responsibly.
- Respect other's rights, beliefs, and opinions even when they do not agree with our own.
- Appreciate and praise law enforcement. Do not judge law enforcement (or any other entity) by the acts of the few, but by the contribution of the many.
- Be mindful of the less fortunate. And rest assured there ARE less fortunate people.

- Preserve one of the most valuable assets known to mankind – the family unit. There is no greater contributor to happiness, success, and peace.
- Take responsibility for our own actions.

It is evident that these groups are not content with being deemed equal but demand preferential treatment because it is their self-granted right. To succumb, would be the beginning of the end of the United States as we know it. Therefore, we, the loyal, law abiding, patriotic citizens of the United States of America, unite in harmony with shared American values and ambitions, do solemnly publish and declare:

- We have the right to free speech and an obligation to permit the same for our fellow citizens.
- We have the freedom to practice religion in our own way and the obligation to allow others the same freedom.
- We have the unalienable right to life liberty and the pursuit of happiness and the obligation to not infringe on anyone else's right to the same.
- We have the right to make the world a better place for ourselves and an obligation to leave the world a better place for our posterity.
- We have no right to infringe on anyone else's rights and the obligation to protect our own.

For the support of this declaration, we mutually pledge to each other our undying allegiance, our unconditional dedication, and our most sincere honor.

My Vision

I hope "Back to the Past" has been entertaining and enlightening. Even more so, I hope that this book will initiate countless productive dialogs. There seems to be a hesitancy among common citizens to have friendly, productive dialog about controversial matters. Too often, controversy ends up with either **agree with me** or **fight**. Within this book, I have intentionally left the reader with many questions and virtually no answers. It would give me great satisfaction to know that this book has generated many such conversations – especially for today's youth and teens and with their elders. If you enjoy this book, please introduce it to your friends and family. Contemplate the embedded questions and derive your own answers. Discuss the issues with your friends and family and especially those with opposing views. Be willing to change your position if the opposition provides a convincing argument, but not without one. Try to get as many people as possible having these conversations. Even if the conversations don't change anyone's position, they are still respectful, open-minded, conversations instead of fights. This is certainly a step in the right direction.

I have a vision of a new breed of unified American patriots.

- Americans who are respectful of all other Americans.
- Americans who are abundantly empathetic and altruistic.
- Americans who appreciate their neighbors and the world we all live in.
- Americans who are willing to compromise for peace and a more perfect union.
- Americans who patiently recognize and appreciate incremental progress toward a future goal.
- Americans who are thankful, forgiving and understanding of our history - not condemning of it.

Thank you for sharing my story. And thank you for propagating conversations. I hope we discover our neighbor's points of view (POV) and that they will understand ours and we will all be on our way to coexisting more peacefully.

www.ingramcontent.com/pod-product-compliance
Lightning Source LLC
LaVergne TN
LVHW050345160826
845677LV00014B/3794